P9-DVX-739

The Best Cat

VALERI GORBACHEV

CANDLEWICK PRESS

Bootsy was the family cat, and everyone loved her.

"Look at our Bootsy," said Grandmother. "She is a real clown."

"Yes!" cried Jeff. "Bootsy is a great clown. She is the best clown in the world!"

"Bootsy can't be a clown," said Ginny.
"She would be afraid of the bright lights
and the loud applause."

"Look at Bootsy now," said Father.
"She is a real football star."

"Yes!" cried Jeff. "Bootsy
is a great football star. She is the
best football star in the world!"

"Bootsy can't be a football star," said Ginny.
"It would be too dangerous."

"Look here," Mother said.
"Bootsy is a real ballerina."

"Yes!" cried Jeff. "Bootsy is a great ballerina. She is the best ballerina in the world!"

"Bootsy can't be a ballerina," said Ginny.
"She wouldn't like wearing a tutu."

"Look at Bootsy now," said Grandfather.
"She is a real fisherman."

"Yes!" cried Jeff. "Bootsy is a great fisherman. She is the best fisherman in the world!"

"Bootsy can't be a fisherman," said Ginny.
"It would be too wet."

"Bootsy is not a fisherman," Ginny declared.
"She is not a ballerina. She is not a football star.
And she is not a clown. Bootsy is just a regular cat."

"But she is a great cat," said Jeff.
"She is the best cat in the world!"

"Yes," Ginny agreed.

"Bootsy *is* the best cat in the world."